This book belongs to

_____

_____

For Madeleine,
Emily and Emilia
L.F.

For Gabriella,
who looks beautiful in pink
K.L.

Sam

Coco

Zebedee

First published in Great Britain in 2009 by Gullane Children's Books
This paperback edition published 2009 by

Gullane Children's Books
185, Fleet Street, London, EC4A 2HS
www.gullanebooks.com

3   5   7   9   10   8   6   4   2

Text © Lulu Frost 2009
Illustrations © Katherine Lodge 2009

The right of Lulu Frost and Katherine Lodge to be identified as the author and illustrator of this
work has been asserted by them in accordance with the Copyright, Designs and Patents Act, 1988.

A CIP record for this title is available from the British Library.

ISBN: 978-1-86233-777-0

Printed and bound in China

Little Honey

Lulu Frost ✴ **Katherine Lodge**

GULLANE
CHILDREN'S BOOKS

Little Honey was going to have a
birthday party. All her friends were invited.
"It's a pink party," she explained, "and you all have to wear pink!"

Little Honey loved pink.

The night before her birthday
Little Honey was so excited
she had a dream . . .

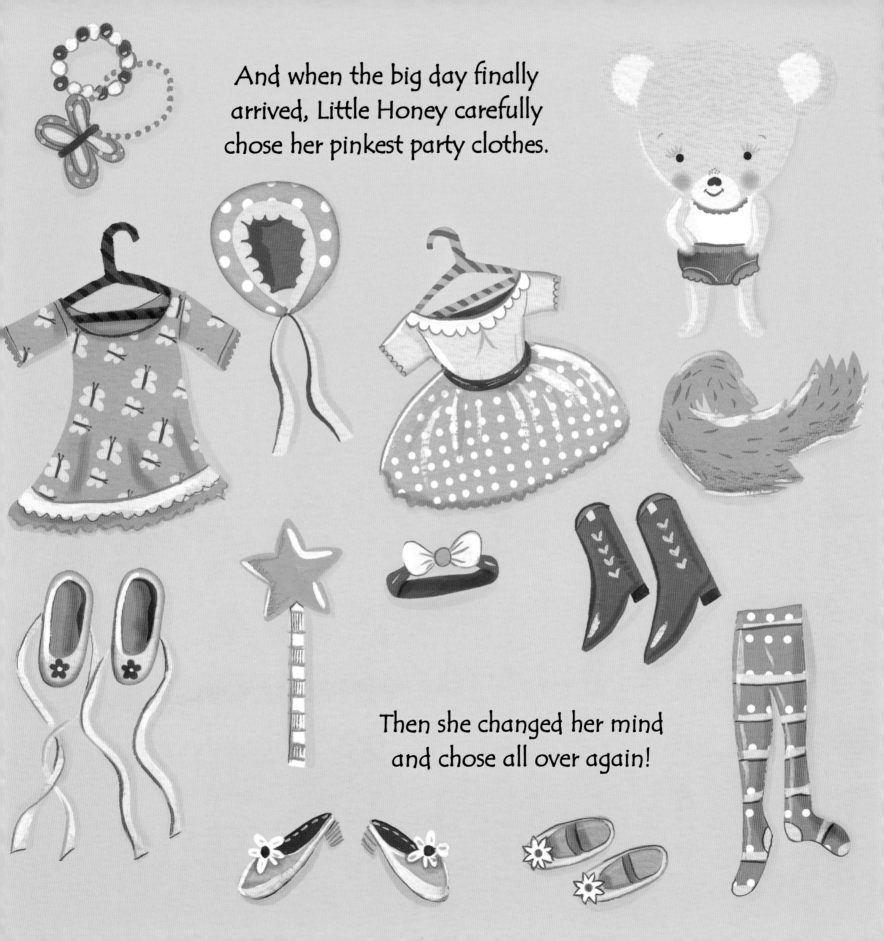

And when the big day finally arrived, Little Honey carefully chose her pinkest party clothes.

Then she changed her mind and chose all over again!

First, Zebedee arrived wearing . . .

GREEN dungarees!
"But I did find pink wrapping
paper," he said. "Happy Birthday!"
"Thank you," said Little Honey.
"I'm sure the others will be wearing pink."

Next, Coco arrived in a princess outfit.

"It *was* pink," she said, "but it turned **RED** in the wash!"

Last was Sam, in **ORANGE!**

"My sister wouldn't let me borrow her pink shirt," he sighed.

"Well, orange is quite nice too," said Little Honey, trying not to sound disappointed.

Little Honey opened her presents.
There was
a skipping rope,
a pencil case and
a sparkly hairbrush!

"Thank you," said Little Honey.
"They are all very nice."
But they weren't pink.

Next, it was time to play some games.
They played Pass the Parcel.

Little Honey won a
PURPLE necklace.
She gave it to Coco.

Then they played Musical Statues and Little Honey won an ORANGE fan. She gave it to Sam.

When they played Hunt the Slipper, Little Honey won a tiny GREEN frog. She gave it to Zebedee.

Little Honey felt sad. The pink party wasn't really pink at all. She remembered her wonderful dream, and a small teardrop tumbled down her cheek.

Coco, Sam and Zebedee ran into the garden to play.

Little Honey didn't
feel like playing any more.
The others didn't seem to notice
her creeping upstairs . . .

Little Honey hadn't been
in her bedroom for long
when there was a whispering and
rustling noise outside the door!

Suddenly, her three friends peeped in.
"Little Honey, we can't have a party
without you," they said.

"But I really wanted a *pink* party,"
sighed Little Honey. Everyone smiled.

"SURPRISE!"

In they marched, all dressed up in . . .

PINK wrapping paper and ribbon!

"It's the PINK Party Parade!
And we made fairy wings for you," said Sam.

"Oh, they're wonderful.
Thank you, *everybody!*"

"So, now it's a pink party after all,"
said Mum, as everyone sat down for tea.
"No," said Little Honey happily. "I do love pink,
but now it's something much, much better. It's a . . .

BEST

FRIENDS PARTY!"

"Three cheers for the
birthday girl!" said Mum.
"Hip, hip hooray!"

Other Little Honey books for you to enjoy...

Little Honey:
Dressing Up Fun!
Katherine Lodge

Little Honey:
Who's Hat's That?
Katherine Lodge

More from Gullane Children's Books . . .

The Secret to Teddy's Happiness
David Conway * illustrated by Dubravka Kolanovic

My Dad!
Charles Fuge

Ten in the Bed
Jane Cabrera

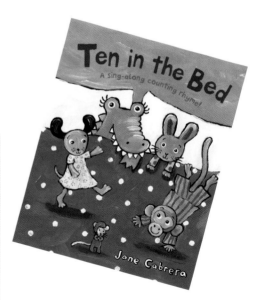